The Guardian's Christmas Confession

P. L. Klein

Crow Quill
Publishing

ISBN: 978-1-0766-6912-4

DEDICATION

To all those who keep Christmas in their hearts.

ACKNOWLEDGMENTS

Thank you to my Beta Readers
Nick, Tracy and Michele.
And Sally who continues to miraculously create
books out of my wild ideas.

CHAPTER 1

June 6, 1944

Gabriel Canfield turned thirty-years-old on June 6, 1944. He celebrated his birthday by storming Omaha Beach with the troops who were part of the amphibious landings. As a medic, he was trained to treat fallen soldiers, to stop the bleeding, sterilize the wound and apply a dressing. Next, he'd administer a sedative and be certain his patient was stabilized before moving on to the next wounded warrior. With a medical background and weeks of intense military field training, Gabriel could do all of those things with ease. There was only one task that deeply troubled him. It was something for which he'd trained, but was convinced he could never be fully prepared for…field triage.

Field triage made sense from a logical perspective. Prioritizing treatment of soldiers who were not mortally wounded increased the numbers of potential survivors. But Gabriel was never comfortable with making those decisions. It felt too much like playing God. Virtually every wounded man on Omaha Beach knew that if the medic passed them by, they were as good as dead…it was just a matter of time. Gabriel would never forget the agony and despair on the faces of the men he passed over to get to those with less serious wounds. There were even times when he stopped long enough to administer morphine to at least make the end less painful.

On Omaha Beach, Gabriel hardly had time to think. He kept moving from one soldier to another helping as many as he could, while trying not to count the number of men he was leaving unattended. Those faces would surely haunt his dreams for the rest of his life.

After moving past one such solder, Gabriel muttered, "God forgive me," and went on to kneel beside another just a few yards up the beach.

"Oh, thank God," the young man moaned.

Shoulder wound. Gabriel sighed, relieved that he could help. There was blood soaking the soldier's uniform, and the young man was in a good deal of pain. He lay there defenseless, unable to hold his rifle, which rested off to his side in the sand.

"I'm just going to clean this out a bit and dress the wound," Gabriel said pulling one of his medical field packs forward.

Gabriel cut a wider opening in the uniform to expose the injury and then went into auto drive. The wound looked clean, though the bullet was clearly still in there. Removing it would have to wait until the young man was evacuated, but Gabriel applied a Carlisle Dressing with sulfa and prepared a syringe of morphine. Just before Gabriel was about to administer the injection, a spray of bullets fell dangerously close sending up a shower of sand. Gabriel managed to keep the grit from contaminating the wound.

"I figured you medics were immune to gunfire," the young man quipped.

"Yeah, you'd think so, wouldn't you?" Gabriel replied while trying to determine where the assault was coming from. "But sometimes I think the Germans think the white crosses on our helmets, arm bands and field bags are just meant for target practice."

Gabriel finished the injection just as another spray of bullets came toward him. Instinctively, he grabbed the soldier's weapon and aimed at the source of the gun fire. An instant later, Gabriel felt a stab of guilt. He was a good shot. Back home on the farm, he'd done well at target practice and hunting. He'd even won a sharpshooter's award at the Grange, but he'd never shot a man before. It never occurred to him that he could willingly hurt someone, which was why he studied medicine and took field medical training. Suddenly, his world had tilted, and he realized he had no idea who he was anymore or what he was becoming. He dropped the gun and with his fingers still trembling, he closed his medical kit and readjusted the harness.

"Someone will be along soon to evacuate you," Gabriel said as he arose and hoisted the medical bags. He kept his head low and put one foot in front of the other, making his way toward his next patient.

Ahead Gabriel saw two infantrymen heading out together. While consciously following them, Gabriel was also keeping an eye out for wounded on the sand.

When the soldiers split up, Gabriel continued to follow the one on the right. There was a deafening roar and Gabriel felt his body tossed into the air and then land hard face up on the sand.

Land mine, Gabriel thought, and instantly realized most of the dead and dying he'd moved past earlier had fallen victim to the mines on the beach, but he felt nothing. No pain whatsoever. He was just considering how lucky he must be, when he glanced down at his chest and saw several wounds that were seeping blood. *And he felt nothing.*

Gabriel recalled classes he'd attended regarding wounds from shrapnel…how sometimes the exterior wound wouldn't even look that bad, but the internal damage was devastating. *And he felt nothing.* Sometimes Gabriel wished he didn't know some of the stuff he knew. This was one of those times. He realized the shrapnel that hit him must have severed his spinal cord as well as tearing up his internal organs. Now he would know first-hand what it felt like to see a medic pass him by. He'd feel the desperate agony of dying alone.

As his blood continued to seep out, a medic did stop. Gabriel recognized him, but didn't know his name. The man was young, and this was his first battle. His face was smeared with grit, smoke and blood as he knelt down next to Gabriel.

"Move on," Gabriel told him. "There's nothing you can do for me."

"Morphine," the young man said while he dug into one of his field packs.

"No, save it," Gabriel whispered. "I don't need it. I don't feel anything."

The medic gave a curt nod, as tears streaked down

his cheeks. He readjusted the harness that held his field packs and moved on just as Gabriel had earlier, whispering, *God forgive me.*

It was a fitting end, Gabriel thought. For all the dying men he'd abandoned in the field, it was oddly appropriate that he should die this way. He closed his eyes, resigned to his fate, but still believing that no one should ever die alone...abandoned.

Somewhere in the distance, Gabriel heard the voice of a little girl singing.

Oh we'll sing the songs of sorrow nevermore, nevermore
Oh we'll sing the songs of sorrow nevermore
We will sail the crystal waters
To the new and shining shore
And we'll sing the songs of sorrow nevermore, nevermore.

Oh we'll sing the songs of sorrow nevermore, nevermore
Oh we'll sing the songs of sorrow nevermore,
We will cross the bridge of memories
That can't hurt us anymore,
And we'll sing the songs of sorrow nevermore, nevermore.

When Gabriel opened his eyes, he saw a beautiful dark-haired girl dressed in a fresh pinafore wearing a crown of wildflowers. At first, he panicked at the sight of an innocent child in the middle of a battlefield, then realized he must be hallucinating...all part of the dying process.

In the carnage and chaos of Omaha Beach, on June 6, 1944, Gabriel Canfield died.

CHAPTER 2

"Come on, Gabriel, come on!"

Gabriel opened his eyes not knowing what to expect, but certainly the young girl with flowers in her hair was the farthest from his mind. This realization was followed by the sensation of walking. He had regained feeling in his body, and he could move. As he made his way down the beach, the sand beneath his feet melted away along with the horrors of battle, and he found himself following the singing girl down a narrow road that cut through a field of wildflowers similar to the blooms that encircled her head.

Oh we'll sing the songs of sorrow nevermore, nevermore...

The song sounded familiar, like a long-lost memory from the life he'd lived before the war. It came from a place of peace and safety. While cherishing that feeling, Gabriel lost sight of the child and found himself at a crossroads with a genial man blocking his way.

"Welcome, Gabriel," the man said inclining his

head slightly. "I'm Duffy, and I'm here to welcome you to the After."

"The After, as in afterlife?" Gabriel asked.

"Ah yes, that is a good sign," Duffy grinned. "Quite often people who pass suddenly or traumatically don't even realize they've passed."

Gabriel listened to the amiable man, but he kept his eye open for the little girl from before.

"Somehow this doesn't match what I was expecting," Gabriel said finally noting the child had headed down the trail to the left and was waving at him from the edge of a wooded area.

"Ah, so you're one of those who expect to see St. Peter, the Pearly Gates, and a choir of angels," Duffy grinned. "Well, we were given to believe you'd be more comfortable with this scene. Less ostentatious, more peaceful. But if you insist, we can certainly roll out the Pearly Gates, and I'm certain Peter wouldn't mind making a personal appearance."

"No, no, that's not necessary," Gabriel assured him. "This will do nicely. So what happens next?"

"Well, there are a list of protocols to be observed to process our new arrivals," Duffy explained. "First, there is the Guardian of Transitions who leads you from life to The After, as our dear Angelica has done for you."

Duffy waved at the child with the flowers in her hair and she joyously waved back, blowing a kiss.

"You know, at the risk of sounding critical again," Gabriel began, "I don't think it's the wisest thing to send a child angel into a battlefield to fetch the dearly departed."

"Oh, but she volunteered," Duffy confided. "She really wanted to come to you at your time. She is usually a guardian who brings the souls down the path of memories to their reunion, but the child is always so eager to please, and she offered to help with transitions."

"But a child in a battle zone is disconcerting," Gabriel insisted.

"I suppose," Duffy agreed. "But Angelica was so persistent. I mean how can you say *no* to that precious child?"

Once again Duffy waved at the giggling child in the distance, and she waved back with both hands.

"Hurry, Gabriel," she shouted, signaling for him to follow her.

"So what now?" Gabriel asked.

"Well, according to the process, I need to determine if you're ready to proceed, or if you should spend time becoming acclimated to your new circumstances."

"I know I'm dead," Gabriel shrugged. "Let's get on with it."

"But sometimes, as I implied before, if you've passed away in a sudden or violent way, there may be some residual negative energy that needs to be dispelled," Duffy explained. He appeared to be nervous about that statement and almost intimidated by Gabriel.

In life, Gabriel had been an imposing figure. He stood six-feet-five-inches tall and was impressively fit. Now in this after life he looked much the same, while Duffy was a slightly plump man of about five and a half feet. But why would a spiritual greeter be afraid of a recently departed dead guy?

"I'm fine," Gabriel insisted. "What happens next?"

"There's no shame in spending time becoming

acclimated to The After," Duffy pointed out.

"If I already know I'm dead and I'm resigned to that then, what's next?" Gabriel demanded.

"It's not just acknowledging your mortal end," Duffy said nervously backing away. "It's also dealing with those adverse parts of our natures that hinder you from fully assuming your spiritual nature."

"I'm here. I'm fine," Gabriel insisted. "Let's just move on."

Reluctantly, Duffy nodded.

"Very well. What comes next is the walk of memories."

A troubled look came to Gabriel's face as he couldn't stop his most recent recollections flooding his mind. He tried to force back the faces of the dying he'd passed by and the fearful anger that had overtaken him as he shot the German sniper. He felt a shiver of guilt run through him, while struggling to remain stoic.

"The newly arrived usually walk through a path of memories," Duffy was saying when Gabriel realized the older spirit was speaking again. Duffy gestured toward Angelica as he went on. "She will lead you through the woodland path, and your life's memories will come to you."

"Uh…no. Not necessary." Gabriel assured him. "I'm quite familiar with my memories and equally content not to relive them."

"But it's part of the protocol," Duffy insisted. "If you don't want the wooded path, you could walk through a garden, over a bridge, or perhaps along a beach."

"*No!*" Gabriel shouted, then realized he may have frightened Duffy, but the last place he wanted to be at this time was on a beach. "No, I don't want to relive memories…at all."

"But it's the way it's done, Gabriel," Duffy said, then as if responding to an unspoken instruction, the small man amended his instruction. "But if you insist, we could forego the memory walk…and perhaps consider a time of acclimation to better adjust to this Afterlife. It will be a time to meditate…"

Gabriel cut Duffy off in mid-sentence.

"Do I look like the sort of person who meditates?" Gabriel asked. "I don't want to relive my past. I just want to move on to what's next."

"Well, what follows the walk of memories is the reunion with all of those you knew who have come to The After before you." Duffy looked troubled when he realized from the emotions playing on Gabriel's face, that he wasn't going to be agreeable to this either.

While considering Duffy's latest revelation, Gabriel realized the only family members he'd have there to greet him were his twin sister, who had been stillborn, and his maternal grandfather who had never approved of his mother marrying his father and despised Gabriel. Then there were all the soldiers who had died as a result of Gabriel passing them by on Omaha Beach and his previous battles, and the German sniper.

"No!" Gabriel said. "I don't need or want that either. What comes next?"

"I don't think you can just skip everything," Duffy said. "I mean there are rules."

"Rules I don't choose to follow," Gabriel stated firmly. "So if that's all you have, then just send me to hell, and be done with it."

Duffy's face paled at the mention of hell, but Gabriel hardly had a chance to take that in before he felt the little girl's hand take his. He jerked free from her and stepped away, but not before he noticed tears welling in her dark eyes.

"We don't say that word here," she stated solemnly.

Gabriel felt properly chastised.

"Perhaps you could give us some privacy, Angelica," Duffy said placing a gentle hand on the child's head.

She nodded and turned away. Her shoulders drooped and she no longer skipped happily away.

Oh we'll sing the songs of sorrow nevermore, nevermore, she sang, only now it sounded more like a dirge.

Oh we'll sing the songs of sorrow nevermore
We'll embrace who went before us
And we'll love them evermore.
Oh we'll sing the songs of sorrow nevermore, nevermore.

As she came to the final word of the song, Angelica evaporated into the mist that had gathered at the path leading into the woods.

"Were you this disagreeable in life?" Duffy asked. His joyous demeaner from before was gone, and he was clearly miffed with Gabriel.

"Yes," Gabriel admitted. "I'm afraid so. I was a huge disappointment to a lot of people which is why I really don't want to relive those memories."

"It's not too late to spend some time getting acclimated," Duffy began. "Or not," he shrugged when Gabriel glared at him.

"The best way for me to deal with my past is to move on," Gabriel insisted. "So what's next?"

"Well, typically after the reunion, one spends some time becoming re-acquainted with their loved ones and then they sometimes choose to do the things they wished they had time to do in life. Some pursue reading the books they never had time to read, or some go fishing or play golf. Some travel and some mentor others here in The After, or they return to the living as mentors." Duffy looked hopeful, clearly wishing that Gabriel had heard something he might like to do.

"How do you mentor the living?" Gabriel wondered.

Duffy was relieved that Gabriel was curious and for once wasn't going to argue with him.

"You know how when you were alive, from time to time, you might hear that little voice in your ear," Duffy grinned. "Well, that was a spirit mentor. Mentors give warnings or words of encouragement. They're never seen, but often heard if a person is listening."

Gabriel did recall hearing voices from time to time. More often than not, he had ignored their good counsel. He doubted he'd be very good at giving advice, and for the most part he wasn't a particularly upbeat person. He just couldn't imagine giving bubbly words of encouragement to some loser.

"You'd be mentoring the living in an area that you're familiar with," Duffy went on. "People who were poets in life encouraging young people who need a word of hope. Spirit artists advise aspiring living artists on design and techniques."

"I'm really not any good at those things," Gabriel shrugged.

"Well, of course not," Duffy smiled. "You might

advise a young person about the military or about medicine. In the heat of battle you would be the calm voice who would keep panicked young medics from making a mistake."

Just hearing the mention of warfare gave Gabriel a pang of guilt.

"No," he whispered, turning away from Duffy. Gabriel had always assumed that if he died, he'd be free of the horrors he'd endured, but now he realized his punishment was not only to die alone and abandoned, but to go through eternity feeling the guilt for deserting the dying in their hour of need.

"Then tell me, Gabriel," Duffy said interrupting Gabriel's thoughts. "What is it that you would prefer to do?"

There was no hesitation in Gabriel's reply.

"I want to do whatever I can to see to it that people are not alone when they pass away," Gabriel said. "I left so many young soldiers dying alone when I knew they were in their final minutes. There were orders…protocols as you say. But I'll never forget the despair I'd seen in their faces. No one should ever be alone when they are dying."

"None of them were alone," Duffy assured Gabriel. "Every one of them was joined by a Guardian of Transition. You couldn't see them, but at the end, I assure, they were not alone."

"Did you send them little girls with flowers in their hair?" Gabriel asked. "That's not what they wanted to see there."

"No, Gabriel, I told you Angelica volunteered to come for you," Duffy explained. "Each dying person is met by a guardian who is assigned to them usually, but Angelica wanted to help."

Gabriel didn't hear the explanation so much as he understood that he could get his wish. He could see to it that no one would have to be alone in their hour of death.

"How do I become one of these Transition guys?" Gabriel asked, eager to get to work.

"Well, a Guardian of Transitions doesn't just sit by the bedside," Duffy began. "They deal in all sorts of transitions, not just life to After. Their task is to guide the living in desperate times when they are experiencing sudden and perhaps traumatic change. They also counsel people who are terminally ill or considering suicide. Or perhaps a person experiencing a divorce or a death of a loved one."

"Okay," Gabriel said considering Duffy's words. "I get it. Being a Guardian of Transition is more than being *The Angel of Death*."

Gabriel noticed Duffy bristle at his comment.

"We don't actually call them *The Angel of Death*," Duffy informed him. "For one thing, you're no angel, and as I told you before, the job description includes more than the transition from life to death. You must accept all assignments, whatever the transition might be. So if you believe you can do that, a mentor will be assigned to you and you can begin."

"Yes. Absolutely. That's what I want."

Since this was the first thing that Gabriel had agreed to, Duffy quickly signaled for a seasoned Guardian to lead Gabriel to his first assignment.

Moments later, a lovely young woman appeared before Gabriel.

"My name is Rachel and I'll be your mentor," she said to Gabriel while she led him past Duffy.

Gazing back, Gabriel noticed Duffy looked

pleased and relieved. As they walked through a peaceful garden, Rachel began her instructions.

"I'm sure Duffy explained what a Guardian of Transitions does, so I'll describe the process so you'll understand what you can expect and how you can use your powers in your work."

"Powers?" Gabriel asked. Did he sound as stupid as he felt?

"As a spirit, you are no longer bound by physical limitations. You will transport spiritually to your assignments. You'll feel a tingling in your hands and feet, and then instantly you'll find yourself where you need to be to meet your next assignment. You'll find it's best to remain invisible until you have assessed the situation, and simply remain what we call *the little voice in their heads.* Depending on the situation, you may have to repeat yourself since those among the living don't always listen or respond."

Gabriel nodded. He understood that firsthand. He made a career of ignoring the voices in his head.

"You will find that you may wish to appear to your client, especially in the case of the dying or the most vulnerable. And always be aware that the client is never under any obligation to listen to you or to obey. While they are in body, they have *free will,* and they make the ultimate decisions for themselves. This is especially important to remember in the case of suicides. In the end, they do have the right to end their lives and we are powerless to stop an act of *free will.*"

Again, Gabriel nodded while trying to concentrate on Rachel's instructions.

"You will have at your disposal anything you need to accomplish your task, except where it may infringe on another's free will," Rachel said.

"What does that mean?" Gabriel asked.

"If a person is dying, they may wish to see someone before they pass," Rachel explained. "Another spirit will be dispatched to *suggest* that the other person might come, but the other is not obligated to go."

"I see," Gabriel said. "*Free will.*"

"Precisely." Rachel smiled and continued. "A Guardian of Transitions is not like a true mentor who might remain with a person for their entire lifetime. We are dispatched for the crisis and then we are assigned to another person who is in a different crisis. Typically we do not spend a lot of time with our clients. We can use whatever material means we need to accommodate our clients with the exception of money."

"Then how do we get whatever we need if we don't use cash?" Gabriel asked.

"Whatever we require is provided. We don't purchase it," Rachel explained. "It's just that when we are helping a client in financial transition, we can't simply give him money to pay or bribe his way out of it. We can suggest ways that person might earn or acquire funds, but we can't hand over a fortune."

That made sense to Gabriel. No one ever handed him a fortune when he incurred expenses for his education, and he managed to work things out.

"It's just about time to begin," Rachel said, as Gabriel began to feel a tingling in his fingers and toes.

Gabriel was mesmerized as he watched Rachel take an exhilarated breath and close her sapphire eyes. He imitated her, and felt the sensation of being lifted off his feet. In the time it took to reopen his eyes, he was in a hospital corridor. A few doors down there was a glow emanating from one of the rooms.

Still a little shaken by his first teleportation, Gabriel held back when Rachel crossed over to the open room. She looked back and motioned for him to join her. A harried orderly walked right through Gabriel as he hesitated in the middle of the hallway.

"Come on, Gabriel," she called. Only he reacted. No one there was aware of their presence.

From within the room he heard the voices of children begin to sing and he was drawn to them.

We will sing the songs of sorrow nevermore, nevermore.
We will sing the songs of sorrow nevermore
We will stroll the garden paths
'Til we reach the golden door
We will sing the songs of sorrow nevermore, nevermore.

It broke Gabriel's heart to see four fearful children standing next to their dying mother's bed singing the song he'd heard earlier. After a moment, Gabriel noticed that only three of the children were singing. The youngest, a boy of about five-years-old was staring at his hands.

"The mother will be my assignment," Rachel whispered, then gestured toward the youngest child. "That is your assignment, Gabriel."

It was only then that Gabriel noticed a glowing light that surrounded the child.

"You'll recognize your clients by their auras," Rachel explained. "We'll wait here until the children leave their mother's bedside. Then I'll go to my client and you'll follow the boy. After that you'll remain unseen until you find an opportunity to make yourself known to him."

Gabriel felt totally unprepared. What did he know about little boys, except the obvious…he had once been one. But this child was about to lose his mother. Gabriel's mother was still alive and well, and likely to find out very soon that he had been killed on Omaha Beach. Gabriel shook himself trying to concentrate on the task at hand. There was no time now to consider how his mother might be grieving his death. There was a small boy who needed to be transitioned in some way. He had no clue what needed to be done. Gabriel envied Rachel who would likely be holding the mother's hand and giving her comfort and companionship prior to leading her into The After.

Clearly the children, especially the youngest, would not be headed for the hereafter any time soon. So what was Gabriel's next move?

"What am I supposed to do?" he called out to Rachel as she was about to enter the hospital room.

"You simply assess the situation, and you'll know in your heart what must be done."

Gabriel had never been a *fly-by-the-seat-of-your-pants* kind of guy, so he wasn't exactly thrilled by this plan. He noticed a group of adults congregated down the hall. They appeared to be discussing the children, so Gabriel drew closer to them.

Within minutes of eavesdropping on the adults, Gabriel had sized up the problem. There were four couples who had been acting as foster parents for the four children and another woman named Endora Sneathen who represented the Chambers Adoption Agency in Carson Creek.

"Of course, we at the Foster Services of Chambers Adoptions appreciate all of your good work with the McKinney children, but when Mrs. McKinney dies, so will your contract as foster parents for your charges." Miss Sneathen's announcement came out as a cold fact, expressing little sympathy for the young ones who were about to lose their mother.

Gabriel angled a little closer to hear the rest of their discussion. When he got a better look at Miss Sneathen, he shuddered to realize with her narrow face, squinty eyes, pointy nose and stubborn jaw, she resembled a wicked witch he'd seen in a movie a few years before.

"Now we all want to see these children settled in favorable homes, so we don't get returns," Miss Sneathen said. "Our orphanage is filled to capacity, so we need to find acceptable permanent homes for them as soon as possible."

The couples appeared to be nice enough people, but none of them looked to be well off.

"You know we'd adopt Franky if we could," one of the men offered. "But we just can't afford another child without the financial help we've been given to be foster parents."

The other adults nodded in agreement.

"Very well," Miss Sneathen said with undisguised impatience. "Then at least tell me some of the good points about your foster child so I'll have something to offer their potential adopted families."

"Families?" one of the foster mothers asked. "But Jenny is of the opinion that if she and her siblings couldn't return to their mother, that at least they'd be all placed in the same home."

"Well, beggars can't be choosers," Miss Sneathen scoffed. "The children will get what they get, and they'll have to be satisfied with that. Now you're the Randolphs aren't you?" she said pointing a boney finger at the first man who spoke.

"Yes, we're the Randolphs and we've been caring for Franky. He's just turned eleven and he's a very studious boy. His mother depended on him to help her, so he's used to hard work. Franky was a big help to me on the farm as well as being dependable and friendly."

Miss Sneathen began to scribble notes on file cards she'd pulled from the fabric tote she placed at her feet.

"Miss Gulch," Gabriel whispered when he recalled the name of the character who Miss Sneathen reminded him of.

"And now the Warners," Miss Sneathen announced as she observed the next card in her collection. "You had Jenny. What can you tell me about her?"

"Jenny is a bright child and very industrious," Mrs. Warner announced. "She's been a great help to me around the house. I had triplets last year and she's been a Godsend with the babies. She's happy to help with cleaning and caring for the triplets and even preparing simple meals. For a nine-year-old she is very mature."

"Ah, good to know," Miss Sneathen said. "If we can't place her in a home, we can put her to work at the orphanage caring for the infants."

Mrs. Warner turned to her husband with a pleading glance.

"You know we can't keep her without the extra money coming in," he whispered. "Maybe we can get another foster child to help you out. A kid who comes with a little cash every month."

"And next are the Dixons," Miss Sneathen

announced, ignoring Mr. Warner's offer. "What can you tell me about Caroline?"

"Carrie is just the sweetest little girl," Mrs. Dixon began. "She's quite the artist and very accomplished for only seven-years-old. Carrie can draw and sing and has been a good help to me around the house. I do know that she dearly misses her siblings though and was given the impression that they would all be together in the end. It would break her heart if they were to be separated permanently."

"Well if it means that much to you, Mrs. Dixon, you and your husband could adopt the lot of them," Miss Sneathen said sneering when the couple demurred.

"And last is the five-year-old," Miss Sneathen said turning to the remaining couple.

"Yes, we're the Lancasters and we have Button," Mrs. Lancaster said.

"That can't be the child's name," Miss Sneathen said referring to her card.

"That's the only name he'll answer to," Mrs. Lancaster explained. "Button is a truly beautiful child, but the death of his father was very traumatizing to him, and I hate to think what his mother's passing will do to him. He is gentle and obedient, but he hasn't said a word since he came to live with us."

"Well, he'll have to get over it," Miss Sneathen snorted. "Come to think of it, a silent child might be just the thing that some couples might want."

"Heartless bitch," Gabriel muttered.

Miss Sneathen glanced around, pinning each couple with her beady eyes. "Did you say something?" she accused.

The rest of the adults shook their heads.

"Did you actually hear me, you wicked old prune?" Gabriel asked.

Miss Sneathen's eyes darted about. She looked behind her and furtively glanced beyond the other adults.

"Didn't you hear that?" she asked. When Gabriel began to laugh, he saw panic on her face. "And that? Do you hear that diabolical laughter?"

When the foster parents all shook their heads in unison, Miss Sneathen composed herself.

"Neither did I," she said stubbornly jutting her pointed chin out as if daring them to contradict her. "Well then let us move into a more private room to sign the termination documents, and then you may leave. I'll be certain to take charge of the children from here on."

"You mean we won't even have the chance to say goodbye to Button?" Mr. Lancaster pleaded.

"I don't see why that would be necessary," Miss Sneathen said as she slipped her note cards in her bag and rummaged around looking for the forms she needed the foster parents to sign.

They all followed Miss Sneathen into a room down the hall, while Gabriel recalled Rachel's last words.

You simply assess the situation, and you'll know in your heart what must be done.

"She was right," Gabriel said. "I know precisely what to do."

And so began Gabriel's afterlife career as a Guardian of Transitions.

CHAPTER 3

December 24, 2019

Gabriel Canfield had been a Guardian of Transitions for seventy-five years. No other in his position had been reprimanded more than he was. The only reason he was still permitted to continue was because when he got it right, he got it spectacularly right. Sadly, when he got it wrong, it was cataclysmically wrong. When new guardians were introduced to the program, Gabriel was used as an example of what *NOT* to do. He was on *probation* for his entire tenure as a Guardian, the longest period ever! There were times when Gabriel took pride in that. His methods weren't always acceptable, but he always got the job done.

The fact was, Gabriel tried not to take it personally. They told him to follow his heart. Was it his fault that his heart had a mind of its own? They knew Gabriel didn't do well with suicides, and yet someone still assigned him suicides. Well then it was their fault if he didn't exactly come across as a nurturing sympathetic spirit. Besides, it was Christmas Eve and that had never been a good time for Gabriel.

Coming from his latest assignment, Gabriel glanced back at the recently departed man he was escorting to Duffy for welcome and assessment.

"Come along, Kirk, I've got someone I want you to meet." In reality, Gabriel was eager to be rid of this idiot, but he wasn't particularly looking forward to Duffy's reprimand. This suicide wasn't handled particularly well, and Gabriel knew it, and pretty much didn't care.

"Oh, what have you done now?" Duffy asked with despair.

"This is Kirk…and he's a jerk," Gabriel announced without apology while pointing back at the rangy looking man who was inordinately interested in Duffy's field of lush wildflowers. "He OD'ed on some concoction of heaven only knows what."

"Did you even try to prevent him from ending his life?" Duffy pleaded.

"Absolutely," Gabriel insisted. "Just not very hard."

"Oh, Gabriel, what are we to do with you?" Duffy gave him a withering look, then became curious as to what was taking Kirk so long to catch up.

Gabriel followed Duffy's gaze and called out again.

"Come on, Kirk, we haven't got all eternity."

"He must really be a wildflower enthusiast." Duffy smiled to think that his preferred reception site was being appreciated for its beauty.

"Not quite," Gabriel sighed. "Kirk is just looking for something he can smoke…preferably something that will get him *freaking high*."

"Oh," Duffy sympathized. "He was addicted in life."

"No, he was a jerk in life," Gabriel complained. "A jerk with a fondness for getting irresponsibly high and with a capacity to be totally oblivious to the horrendous misery he left in his wake."

"You really should work on your ability to empathize with humanity," Duffy suggested.

"Oh really?" Gabriel asked. "You be the judge."

"We don't judge," Duffy pointed out.

"Okay, so you don't judge him, but you do judge my attitude," Gabriel countered, glaring at Duffy with a raised brow.

"I merely suggest you could improve your performance if you'd be a little less impatient," Duffy said eyeing Kirk again.

"Front and center," Gabriel called back to Kirk. "My friend, Duffy, wants to ask you a few questions and assess your fitness to cross over into the afterlife. But first he's going to let you cool your heels a bit to get rid of your negative tendencies."

"Gabriel, that's not your decision to make," Duffy scolded.

"Oh, Duffy, my friend, this guy is going to make even you lose your patience," Gabriel boasted.

Gabriel jogged back and physically pushed Kirk up to Duffy.

"This is Kirk," Gabriel announced. "I found him in his wife's mobile home about to consume a fistful of her anti-anxiety pills and wash them down with a quart of whiskey. At least I think it was whiskey. It was some concoction he made up in his own still."

Duffy shook his head while noticing that Kirk was wandering off again to check out the wildflowers.

"Kirk's wife works days in a bar and grill as a cocktail waitress. Our friend here married her because she makes *freaking good tips* and she's willing to support this lazy creep."

"I have a condition," Kirk called over his shoulder. "I can't work. I'm a *gory phoby something or other*."

"Agoraphobic," Duffy concluded. "Well that must have been a challenge in your life. No wonder you were depressed and fell prey to alcohol and suicidal tendencies."

"You haven't heard the whole story yet," Gabriel grinned. "It seems Kirk got his wife pregnant."

"And I've never been fond of pregnant women," Kirk chimed in. "They get fat and hemorrhoidal."

"I think he means hormonal," Duffy suggested.

"It could go either way," Gabriel shrugged.

"Let's just say she was less attractive to me," Kirk added.

"So naturally, he started looking for extramarital entertainment and decided to hit on his wife's friend from work."

"Oh dear," Duffy said.

"And he entertained the other waitress during the day while his wife was working," Gabriel explained. "Apparently, his agoraphobia didn't bother him at all when he was taking his lady friend out during the day."

"Well them symptoms comes and goes," Kirk said with a lecherous wink.

"So one day Kirk decided to entertain said waitress at home…his wife's home…in his wife's bed." Gabriel made it clear he was pretty disgusted with Kirk's behavior. "And that was the day his wife came home early and found our Romeo with his Juliet. And

Juliet had just announced she too was pregnant."

"Oh dear," Duffy repeated.

"When Kirk's wife found out, she kicked him out," Gabriel continued. "But instead of apologizing, this idiot had an ingenious idea. He decided to pretend he was so remorseful that he would attempt suicide, believing that both of those women would feel sorry for him and take him back."

"It was *freaking* inspired," Kirk announced clearly impressed by his logic.

Both Gabriel and Duffy were incredulous as they eyed Kirk's pride.

"Kind of makes you wonder what voices he's hearing in his head, doesn't it?" Gabriel said under his breath.

"Come on," Kirk insisted. "Women are soft in the head and heart for a needy guy like me. If I could pull this off, both of those ladies would have been doing whatever I wanted. I'd have a wife to support me and a girlfriend to help with the expenses, and with them both working and ballooning out, I'd have time to find a new girlfriend. I had it all planned."

Gabriel couldn't help but notice Duffy's shock.

"And that amazing scenario would have actually come to pass, at least in his opinion, if he only hadn't miscalculated his body's tolerance for an old prescription of antianxiety pills and a bottle of hard liquor," Gabriel grinned.

"Please tell me you at least tried to stop him," Duffy pleaded.

"I told him not to, but clearly he wasn't about to listen when he had such a *freaking inspired plan*," Gabriel explained.

"And it really worked!" Kirk bragged. "And this is

a freaking super hallucination. I can't wait to tell my wife and girlfriend how I nearly died and went to heaven."

"I told you he was going to need a little time getting acclimated," Gabriel grinned.

A moment later, Gabriel felt the now familiar tingling in his fingers and toes.

"Oops. Gotta go!" Gabriel announced.

"Yeah, I almost forgot. It's Christmas Eve," Duffy said turning Kirk towards the acclimation center. "The holidays are always a busy time for us."

Gabriel closed his eyes and felt himself transported to a home in the suburbs of Carson Creek. There was a gas fire glowing in the fireplace in a room that looked as if Santa's elves had personally covered every surface with holiday decorations.

"I don't want you wrecking that electric thingy we're giving to Joey," an older woman said to the man in the room.

Moving back to the corner, Gabriel waited to assess the situation. He already knew that his next client was the man who had an aura glowing about him.

"Seriously, Stan. I don't want you to do anything to it," the woman said as she wrapped a bright red scarf around her neck and shrugged into her winter coat. "I really think Joey is too young for electronic doohickeys."

"Nonsense, Polly," Stan insisted. "That boy is just as old as I was when I started getting electric kits. After all these years they've taken all of the excitement out of these things. All kinds of safety features. There's hardly any thrills left in these kits anymore."

Stan peeled off the plastic seal and emptied the contents of the box on the table before him. While he sorted through the contents, he shook his head with disappointment. Then his eyes began to sparkle. Clearly the old fellow had an idea.

"This kit clearly needs some modification," Stan announced, which brought a weary frown to his wife's face.

"Oh, please, Stan, don't break it before Joey even opens it," she lamented.

"I won't break anything. I know what I'm doing."

Famous last words, Gabriel said.

"Famous last words," Polly repeated. "I mean it, Stan. By the time I get back from the store, all those parts had better be back in the box, because I need to wrap it and have it under the tree before the kids come over for dinner."

"Ya ya ya," Stan said waving her off. "All I'm going to do is snap a few things together and test the circuits and maybe up the voltage a little."

"No, you don't," Polly protested checking her pockets for her car keys. "Remember, you've got a pacemaker. You can't just laugh off those random shocks you used to get. Promise you will only look and not start plugging stuff in or doing one of your stupid modifications."

"I know what I'm doing, woman," Stan insisted.

No you don't, Gabriel said.

"No you don't," Polly repeated. "I'm serious. Put all those things back in the box and leave it be."

Polly stood next to the table glaring at him until he impatiently scooped all of the items spread out on the surface, and tucked them back into the box. Once he finished his task, she snatched the box and took it to a stack of gift-wrapping supplies. She found some wrapping tape and sealed the box with it, then left it near the Christmas wrapping area.

"Now, while I'm gone, you'd better make yourself useful," Polly suggested. "You could get down my punch bowl and be sure there's clean towels in the guest bathroom. And maybe you could vacuum up pine needles around the tree."

"It's a fake tree," Stan grumbled. "How can there be pine needles?"

"The thing still sheds," Polly complained. "Unless you want to go out and do the last-minute shopping and face all of those half-crazed shoppers."

"No, no, no," Stan said already getting the stepstool to reach up to the high cupboard to get the punch bowl.

"I'll be back very soon," Polly said waiting for Stan to climb down with her punch bowl before she planted a tender kiss on his cheek. "Be good while I'm gone, and I'll make you some hot cocoa when I return. And don't tackle that snow in the driveway. The plow service will be here in an hour. There's no sense in risking your heart when the young guys can clear out that snow in no time."

"You're such a worrier, Polly," Stan said as he gave her cheek a peck.

You need someone to look after you, Gabriel said.

"You need someone to look after you, Stan." Polly said as she made her way to the door.

"I'm happy it's you who does it, Polly," Stan winked.

Polly giggled as she threw Stan a kiss from the doorway. Stan playfully pretended to catch it and tuck it in his plaid shirt pocket.

As soon as Polly left, Stan marched over to the stash of gift wrap and reclaimed the box he'd opened earlier.

Maybe you should change those towels in the guest bathroom, Gabriel suggested.

"There's plenty of time to do that later," Stan answered. "Polly's going to be gone for hours fighting the crowds in the store and the traffic on the highway."

Stan brought the electric kit over to the table where the light was better and pried off the recently applied tape.

"Polly will never know how I improved Joey's gift."

Oh, I have a feeling she'll know, Gabriel said. *How about vacuuming the floor like Polly asked, and it would be really helpful if you'd wash the dishes as well.*

Stan looked across the kitchen to the stack of dirty dishes in the sink and on the nearby counter.

"You're right, Polly's been busy all day preparing food for the dinner tonight," Stan said.

She'd really appreciate your help, Gabriel insisted.

Indecision struck Stan as he eagerly eyed the mass of parts lying before him on the table and stacks of dishes in the sink.

Forget about the kit. Do the dishes. Vacuum the floor.

"Oh, I can do all that," Stan said sorting through the collection of parts on the table. He started humming a Christmas carol as he studied the pieces from the box, then jumped up from his seat and ran to a bottom drawer near the sink. After rooting around in the spare parts left over from previous projects, Stan came back to the table with plugs and frayed cords, as well as a cord splicer and some electrical tape.

Don't do it, Stan, Gabriel warned as he sensed a new danger. *Stan, you know you've been having chest pains recently. Your pacemaker is defective. Even a slight shock could be fatal to you.*

Stan paused for a moment considering Gabriel's last warning. Then he shook his head, dismissing the voice in his ear and resumed his project. Apparently, the voice in his ear wasn't enough.

Gabriel slowly let himself materialize before the old man, hoping the shock of seeing a spirit appear before him wouldn't be enough to cause a heart attack.

"Who are you?" Stan asked, as if spirits spontaneously showed up all the time.

"I'm Gabriel, and I'm here to warn you that what you are doing could bring about your death."

Stan squinted at Gabriel, sizing him up. Gabriel stood his ground realizing when he'd finished convincing Stan to give up his experiment, he'd have to erase Stan's memory so that he'd have no recollection of a spiritual visitation.

"Gabriel?" Stan finally said. "Gabriel as in the angel Gabriel? Are you *The Angel of Death*?"

"Actually, the angel Gabriel of the Bible is the angel of Annunciation," Gabriel clarified. "And there really is no *Angel of Death per se*. I'm a Guardian of Transitions and right now you need to make the decision to put this project away and forget about your experiments, or you will very likely die."

"But you're not actually *The Angel of Death*, right?" Stan asked.

Gabriel was becoming impatient. The little voice in the ear hadn't worked and neither had a spiritual intercession. What would it take for Stan to abandon his potentially deadly activity?

"No, I'm not *The Angel of Death*, but the Guardian of Transitions is essentially the same thing," Gabriel insisted.

"But you're not the actual *Angel of Death*," Stan repeated, "and I'll bet you're not an electrician either."

"No, I'm not," Gabriel acknowledged. "But I have a medical background and I've seen what it looks like when a person gets electrocuted. And I know that it would take very little to short out your pacemaker…much less than it would take to electrocute a regular healthy person."

"But you're not an electrician," Stan repeated. "I know what I'm doing."

Gabriel turned away in frustration, trying to come up with another method of discouraging Stan, but he was happily plugging things in and setting off sparks right up to the point that he clutched his chest and fell from his chair. An instant later, Polly burst through the door.

"Silly me," she said, at first not noticing Stan on the floor. "I left without my shopping list."

No longer visible, Gabriel ached to see Polly's grief when she realized Stan was on the floor. She ran to the phone to call for help, then rushed to his side to begin CPR. Since Stan was somehow still clinging to life, Gabriel remained there and joined Polly in the ambulance as they sped to the hospital.

St. Luke's Mercy Hospital was a regular stop for Gabriel. It was the site of his first assignment, seventy-five years before. This was a good hospital, but there was only so much one could do. The doctors worked feverishly to keep Stan alive as Polly went in the hallway. Gabriel noticed an aura form around Polly and Rachel appeared, wrapping a comforting arm around the bereft woman. When the doctors left, Gabriel noticed an elderly priest hurry in to give Last Rites to Stan. Gabriel entered the room with the priest and watched Stan's spirit arise from the bed leaving only his body behind while the old priest recited the prayers for the dead and dying.

I thought you said you weren't The Angel of Death, Stan said though the priest was totally oblivious to their conversation.

What I said was that I am a Guardian of Transitions which is essentially the same thing.

Well, if you'd made that a little clearer maybe I wouldn't have ended up here, Stan said fixing Gabriel with an accusing glare.

This one is not on me, Gabriel insisted. *You had final say in what you were doing.* Free Will. *You chose to act even though I warned you not to.*

Stan's spirit paced the room while the priest began to chant some prayers and Gabriel became concerned about the priest's labored breathing.

What am I supposed to do now? Stan asked. *Polly's going to be all alone. And she'll be pissed too. She warned me not to mess with that electric kit.*

Gabriel noticed the priest make the sign of the cross on Stan's forehead while wincing in pain.

You're having a heart attack, Gabriel spoke to the priest who looked about to find the source of the voice. *You need to speak to a doctor immediately,* Gabriel added.

"Yes, I do," the priest said as he slowly shuffled out of the room clutching his chest.

Gabriel longed to help the priest, but he hadn't

seen his aura, so the priest was not his concern. He knew that the protocols declared that his next act was to escort Stan to Duffy for welcome and assessment.

Gabriel accompanied Stan out into the hall where they both saw a brokenhearted Polly receive word from the cardiologist that Stan had passed away. Farther down the hall, Gabriel saw the priest speaking to a nurse, who rushed to bring a wheelchair to him, while another nurse summoned a doctor to help the priest. Gabriel had seen the priest before administering the sacraments at St. Luke's. In the last fifteen years, the old priest had been one of the chaplains at the hospital. Gabriel knew the priest was compassionate and well-loved and respected at St. Luke's.

Keeping one eye on the priest and one on Stan kept Gabriel distracted until the priest was wheeled into a room down the hall.

What's my Polly going to do now? Stan asked.

She'll have to move on alone, Stan. Gabriel tried to sound sympathetic and realistic at the same time. *She'll have your children and grandchildren to help her.*

If I could only speak to her one more time, Stan said with earnest regret.

What would you tell her, Stan? If you tell me, I can relay the message to her, Gabriel said.

Tell her I love her and I'm sorry I didn't listen to her. Stan said leaning in to kiss her once more on the cheek. *And tell her not to give my fishing gear to her brother.*

Gabriel relayed the message, and moments later her family members arrived to bring her some solace.

It's time to go, Gabriel said placing a hand on Stan's shoulder. A moment later, Gabriel was leading Stan up to Duffy who was waiting near his field of wildflowers.

"Duffy, I'd like you to meet Stanley Kozal, whose cause of death was failure to listen to his wife," Gabriel announced. "And he ignored my advice as well."

"Gabriel," Duffy warned.

"It's true," Stan admitted. "If I'd paid attention to Polly, I'd probably still be alive."

"Well, he actually also had a bad heart and a faulty pacemaker," Gabriel conceded. "He's kind of a likeable idiot, and he loved a good woman who was a saint to have put up with him for as long as she did."

"Gabriel," Duffy admonished again.

"No, that's true," Stan agreed again. "I didn't deserve my Polly. What's she going to do without me? What will I do without her? How I hate to leave her on Christmas Eve."

"She's going to be just fine," Duffy assured him. "And as for you, this lovely young child will escort you down the path of memories."

Gabriel noticed Angelica appear with her winsome look. She grinned and waved at Gabriel before she linked arms with Stan and urged him toward the path leading through the woods. Gabriel hadn't seen Angelica for a while and wondered what had brought her back again.

"We're going to take a nice walk and remember all the wonderful things that have happened in your life," Angelica said to Stan. "And at the end of the trail is a lovely archway. When you pass under it, you'll meet all of your friends and family who went before you."

"And my pets too?" Stan asked. "I read someplace that we might see our pets too."

"Yes," Angelica giggled. "Pets too. I just love the

pets."

"Oh, I'm so grateful," Stan enthused. "Now I'll get the chance to see my old hunting dog, Scrapps, and tell him how sorry I was that I shot him by mistake when we went out hunting rabbits. Polly got so mad at me for that."

Stan's voice trailed off as he and Angelica proceeded down the trail.

"Idiot," Gabriel grumbled. "Polly is truly a saint."

Duffy nodded in agreement.

"Oops, gotta go," Gabriel said. "I'm feeling tingly again."

CHAPTER 4

Gabriel was back at St. Luke's Mercy Hospital, and this time the priest had an aura. Seeing the priest in bed hooked up to an IV and a heart monitor saddened the guardian. The priest's life was very likely coming to an end and all of the holy man's comforting good works at St. Luke's would end as well.

From his place in the corner of the room, Gabriel observed the priest, sitting up looking better as he conversed with a younger man with a briefcase.

"You'll be able to make those additions to my will very soon, won't you?" the priest asked.

"Sure, Uncle Drew," the young man replied while placing loose papers in his briefcase. "I'll just make the adjustments on my computer and print out your new will at the library next door and be back later for your signature."

"I know you don't usually do probate work, Timothy," the old priest grinned. "I really appreciate you making an exception for your old uncle."

"No problem, Uncle Drew." Timothy smiled. "I'll see you later."

When the attorney left, so did the benevolent smile on the priest's face. It was replaced by a grim expression of worry and a slight grimace of pain. A moment later, the priest looked up with a pleasant expression of surprise.

"I know who you are," he said surprising Gabriel who hadn't intended to show himself just yet.

"You can see me?" Gabriel asked.

"Oh yes," the priest grinned. "And I've been expecting you. I'd know you anywhere. Your reputation precedes you."

Gabriel gave the priest a quizzical look. He couldn't imagine what the priest was referring to.

"I've been at St. Luke's for about fifteen years now, and I've heard tell of you since the very beginning," the priest enthused. "The patients and their families always speak of the large man with the deep voice who gives kindly words of comfort and encouragement. Nurses even speak of seeing apparitions of you in the halls and rooms late at night...sitting with the dying in the wee hours after family and loved ones have departed for the night. They tell me that you are always here to be certain no one dies alone."

"I guess I never realized so many people noticed," Gabriel admitted.

"They call you the *Kindly Angel of Death*," the priest said. "I feel truly blessed to have made your acquaintance."

The priest gave a slight bow in acknowledgement of Gabriel's presence and gestured for him to take a seat next to the bed.

"I'm Father Andrew, Father Drew for short," the old priest said with a playful glint in his eye. From the look of him now, Gabriel would never guess that the old man was dying.

"I'm Gabriel, and I'm not *The Angel of Death*," Gabriel admitted. "And there are some that would say I'm not particularly kind either. What I am is a spirit…a Guardian of Transitions and part of my job is to escort the departed to The After."

"Ah yes," Father Drew sighed. "I recall hearing your voice earlier, advising me to consult a doctor."

"Yes, that was me," Gabriel said taking a chair. "I'm pleased you took my advice. You'd be amazed how many don't."

"Well, I confess, I'm just about ready," Father Drew said with a long sigh. "It's hard to leave this beautiful life, but I'm in the business of believing in a better afterlife. I do hope you're not here to tell me otherwise."

"Not at all," Gabriel assured the priest. "I believe you will be favorably impressed."

"Would it be possible to wait until my nephew returns with my new will?" Father Drew asked.

"That's not my call," Gabriel told him. "But I'll be here with you, however long it takes. So we can just relax and talk for a while, or you can rest."

"Oh let's talk," Father Drew glowed with enthusiasm. "I do love to talk, and I have so many questions for you. I'm curious about what to expect and wondering what I'll be doing after I've passed away."

"After you pass, I'll escort you to a greeter named Duffy," Gabriel began only to be interrupted by the priest.

"What? Not St. Peter?"

"I wondered the same thing when I died," Gabriel said enjoying that the priest and he shared the same question. "And if you really want St. Peter, Duffy can arrange it, but Duffy's welcome is most beautiful…a field of wildflowers and a path that leads into a wooded glen.

"Yes, that does sound peaceful," Father Drew agreed. "Then what?"

"Duffy determines if you're ready for The After or if you may require some time to deal with any negative aspects of your life or character, but I wouldn't worry about that if I were you," Gabriel said with a shrug. "If they accepted me, you have nothing to worry about."

Father Drew leaned back onto his fluffed-up pillows that supported his back, and breathed a subtle sigh of relief.

"Then another spirit will escort you down the path of memories and at the end you'll meet all of your loved ones who have passed before you."

"How wonderful," Father Drew enthused.

It occurred to Gabriel that the priest was more eagerly looking forward to the protocols than Gabriel had been.

"At my age, so many of my family members and friends have pre-deceased me," the priest admitted. "It will be such a treat to be together with them again."

"Yes, I'm sure it will," Gabriel said envying the old man.

"And then what happens after that?" Father Drew asked.

Gabriel was taken aback for a moment. No one

ever before had asked him what happened after the reunion part. Surely, they ultimately found out and made their choices, but none had bothered to ask once they reached the part about being reunited with their family and friends.

"I mean, I assume we all do something for the rest of eternity," Father Drew went on. "And of course I have some ideas."

"Really?" Gabriel asked. "What sort of ideas?"

"Well, for a lot of years I was a parish priest." Father Drew grinned at the memory. "Don't get me wrong, I loved it, but when the job became too much and I got too old to keep up, I retired to become chaplain here at St. Luke's."

Father Drew nodded as an even broader smile came to his face.

"I think I'd like to do what you do, Gabriel," Father Drew went on. "I loved being chaplain here and I suspect what you do and how you do it is a lot like being a chaplain."

After Gabriel's initial shock, he knew he had to set Father Drew straight on the expectations of a Guardian of Transitions.

"First of all, I'm about the furthest thing from a chaplain," Gabriel admitted. "And a Guardian of Transitions helps with more than just the peaceful deaths in hospitals. Just today, I had to transition a man who committed suicide, and another who accidentally electrocuted himself."

"And I prayed over both of those men," Father Drew said solemnly. "I was also a chaplain in the military during the Vietnam War, and a parish priest in an inner-city church before coming to St. Mary's Parish in Carson Creek, so I'm no stranger to violence."

Gabriel was humbled by the priest's admission. Finally, he looked up to the priest who now looked hopeful.

"I'm not the person who makes assignments," Gabriel said. "All I know is they certainly take into account what you want to do and what you have a gift for, so they'd probably be delighted to have you become a Guardian of Transitions."

"But what do *you* think, Gabriel?" Father Drew pleaded. "Do *you* believe I've got what it takes?"

"Yes, I do," Gabriel said thinking the old priest was probably better suited to the task than Gabriel was himself.

"Would you mind telling me what you do?" Father Drew asked. "I mean I realize you dealt with a suicide and accidental death already today, and now I'm about to cash in my chips. Is this what I can expect?"

"Every day is different," Gabriel explained. "And many transitions do not include death. In the case of suicides, we try to be the voice of reason and talk them out of it, but ultimately the person will do as they wish because they have free will."

The priest nodded in acknowledgement.

"And in the case of the man who died accidentally, I gave him dire warnings right up until the end, but he refused to listen," Gabriel said wondering if the priest would have been any more successful at preventing those earlier deaths.

"I'm curious about the transitions you spoke about that don't involve death," Father Drew said.

Gabriel considered his answer as he tried to recall the countless transitions he'd facilitated over the previous seventy-five years. They all seemed to run together in a career that involved thousands of people over the years.

"So many," Gabriel said shaking his head at the enormity of those numbers.

"Then tell me your first," Father Drew said. "Do you remember the first transition you ever performed?"

Gabriel felt a peaceful calm descend upon him. His first transition happened decades before, but it still remained fresh in his mind. It would always hold a special place in his heart, and those children would forever remain young in his memory.

"I had died on Omaha Beach on D-Day," Gabriel began. "I was a medic. There were medical protocols that ordered medics to treat wounded soldiers who stood the best chance of survival and leave those with what were categorized as terminal injuries."

Gabriel felt the priest gentle gaze upon him and had to rise and turn away as he admitted his actions on the field of battle.

"I lost track of the number of soldiers I treated that day," Gabriel admitted. "I couldn't pick them out of a lineup. But I remember the faces of the men I left behind. The ones I couldn't help. And every one of them were pleading for me to stay…to give them the hope that they weren't dying. If they saw the medic walk past without helping them, they knew they were considered terminal. All I could do is move on to the next viable wounded soldier and beg for God's forgiveness for letting the others die."

"War is indeed hellish," the priest whispered. "I have a feeling that God suffers even more than we do in those times."

While appreciating Father Drew's kind words,

Gabriel could still feel the raw guilt after all those years.

"I met a just end on the field of battle," Gabriel went on. "I was near a soldier who tripped a landmine, and was hit by shrapnel. From what I could tell, I had a severed spinal cord and other internal injuries and I was bleeding out while other medics passed me by."

"I'm sorry," the priest whispered with heartfelt sympathy.

"A fitting end though," Gabriel grinned sadly as he turned back to the priest. "Don't you think? I mean, after all those poor souls I'd left behind myself?"

"I believe that was simply a coincidence of battle," Father Drew said. "I can't believe there was a vindictive act of retribution because you were unable to treat those who were mortally wounded."

"I wish I felt that," Gabriel said then paused before he continued. "I killed a man that day as well. At the end, the way I died, I believe I deserved it. Anyway, a child came to the battlefield and led me to Duffy, and I told him that I didn't feel anyone should die alone, and that's how I chose to spend my eternity."

"After your memory walk and reunion," the priest assumed out loud.

"No," Gabriel corrected him. "With the battlefield and those dying soldiers so fresh in my mind, the last thing I wanted to do was to indulge in memories. And the only other people who had died before me were my twin sister who was stillborn and my mother's father who despised me. I just skipped all that and started to become a Guardian of Transitions. I was assigned a mentor named Rachel who is very beautiful and extremely patient. She explained the rules and then we began our first assignment."

"And what are the rules," Father Drew asked as Gabriel was seated again.

"Oh things like you remain invisible until you've assessed the situation," Gabriel explained. "You can be the voice in their head or become visible like I am now. Another rule is that you can make suggestions, but you can't force people to do what they wouldn't ordinarily choose for themselves."

"Free will," Father Drew said nodding in understanding.

"That's right," Gabriel said. "Also, a Guardian of Transitions isn't permitted to remain indefinitely. By definition we're meant to help for a limited time, and while we're meant to help in times of crisis, and we have many resources at our disposal, we can't just give people a bunch of money to solve their problems."

"That makes sense," Father Drew agreed.

"Yeah, but it sure would come in handy when a family is about to be removed from their property and the sheriff arrives along with the banker," Gabriel explained. "And then the guy takes the banker and the sheriff hostage and threatens to kill them unless the bank stops foreclosure proceedings on his farm."

"That happened?" Father Drew asked with disbelief.

"Oh yeah," Gabriel grinned.

"What did you do?" the priest asked.

Gabriel instantly regretted using that story as an example when he recalled how he got out of that standoff.

"Well?" Father Drew repeated.

"You know how I said that we have access to whatever we need to complete our task?"

The priest nodded.

"Well, one of those things is sometimes the ability to see people as they really are including their less than honorable activities," Gabriel admitted. "I got the image of the banker in a compromising position with one of his bank tellers and a little voice in his ear informed him that if he proceeded with the foreclosure, his wife would find out about the affair."

"Oh dear," the priest gasped. "I don't suppose I could ever do that."

"Yeah. I wasn't supposed to do that either," Gabriel admitted. "But I figured they shouldn't have given me the visual if they didn't want me to use it."

"But that's extortion," Father Drew said.

"And don't think I didn't hear about it from my boss."

"Was the farmer your first assignment?" the priest asked.

"Oh no," Gabriel grinned. "My first assignment was something totally different. It was a very sad situation, but I think it turned out rather well, if I do say so myself."

Father Drew relaxed as Gabriel began to tell the tale of his first client.

"My first experience as a Guardian of Transitions began right here at St. Luke's seventy-five years ago. It involved a family...a mother and her four children. Their father was killed in the war and their mother was dying. Each of the children had been in a different foster home prior to the mother's death, but when she died, they were to be taken to the Chambers Adoption Agency. This woman named

Endora Sneathen was their caseworker. She was this ugly mean-spirited old hag who had no intention of keeping the children together, even though the agency had promised their mother her children would be kept together, and the four sets of foster parents had been telling the children they'd be reunited."

"What did you do?" Father Drew asked.

"Rachel had told me that I'd know what to do as soon as I'd observed all the facts and assessed the situation, but I had my doubts," Gabriel confessed. "My assignment was specifically the youngest one, a five-year-old named Button, but I knew I couldn't help that boy without also involving his older siblings."

A smile of satisfaction spread across the old priest's face as he silently urged Gabriel to continue.

As Gabriel began to tell the tale, he found himself transported back to that day, reliving the events from so long ago.

CHAPTER 5

June 1944

Gabriel stood in the corridor of St. Luke's as the children left their mother's room. Franky, the oldest, stood stoically as his younger sisters wept on his shoulders. Button dragged his feet coming out, looking as if he were lost in thought, unable to comprehend that he'd just lost his mother. Instead of joining the others, he stood apart studying something in his hand.

In an instant, Gabriel knew what he had to do for the children, he just wasn't too clear on how he was going to achieve it. Since an aura still glowed around the youngest, Gabriel knew that Button was the key to his solution.

"What do you have there, pal?" Gabriel asked.

The child held his hand out palm up to show Gabriel a leather button with a wire loop in the back. When Gabriel leaned in for a closer look, the child closed his hand into a tight fist and shoved it into his pocket.

"Leave him alone, mister," Franky said as the other children joined him to protect their baby brother.

"You're the McKinney children, aren't you?" Gabriel asked which surprised the oldest child.

"How do you know our last name?" Franky demanded as he pulled his younger brother close.

"My name is Gabriel," he announced while holding his hand out to the older child to shake, but Franky simply stared at it until Gabriel drew it back. "I'm here to find a home for you."

"That's what Miss Sneathen is doing," Franky said on behalf of the others, who nodded in agreement…all except the youngest who was distracted once more by his button.

"Yes, well she's very busy in a meeting with your foster parents right now," Gabriel explained as he glanced back at the room where Miss Sneathen and the foster parents were supposed to be signing termination documents. That surely wouldn't take long, so Gabriel knew that if he were to intercept the McKinney children it had to be now or never.

"Has Miss Sneathen found a new family for us?" Jenny asked with hopeful tears in her eyes. It broke Gabriel's heart to see her trying so hard to blink back her sorrow.

"Yes…well, Miss Sneathen hasn't had much luck finding a family for you all, but I think I have a plan," Gabriel said to four pairs of skeptical McKinney eyes.

"What kind of a plan?" Franky demanded as he hugged the other children tighter around him.

"Since Miss Sneathen can't find a family that will take all four of you," Gabriel explained, "I believe I'll be able to locate a place that is willing to take you all, and isn't that what we all want?"

The girls nodded hopefully, but Franky was doubtful.

"What do you know about us, and what makes you think you can find a family for us if Miss Sneathen can't?" Franky demanded.

"Well, I know you were on a farm recently with the Randolphs," Gabriel said addressing Franky. "Mr. Randolph told Miss Sneathen that you were good help on his farm and this place I know about is a farm."

There was barely a twitch of a smile that Franky immediately hid. "What else?" he demanded.

"Well, I heard Jenny's been a good helper at the Warners' house and that she's good at cooking and cleaning and that farm could also use some indoor help. The woman's real nice and a pretty good cook herself. Jenny could learn a lot from her."

"And what about me?" Carrie asked shyly.

"Well, the Dixons had lots to say about how beautifully you sing and how artistic you are," Gabriel said directly to the younger girl. "I happen to know that the farmer loves to sing, and his wife plays piano and gives lessons."

Carrie looked up hopefully to her older brother, who remained suspicious.

"What can they do for Button?" Franky demanded.

"I don't know," Gabriel admitted. "Do you know why he doesn't talk or why he's so taken with that button?"

"He hasn't spoken since he found out our dad died," Jenny said reaching out to stroke her younger brother's hair. "When we said goodbye to our dad before he joined the army, the button on his winter coat fell off and he gave it to Button to keep safe until he got home."

"Dad said Button should use that coat button to remember him while he was gone," Carrie said. "The coat button was meant to remind Button that he was never alone."

"Then Dad got killed," Franky said picking up the story. "Since then, Button hasn't said a word. Now that Mom's died, we need to stick together. We have to protect Button."

Gabriel's heart ached to hear about the five-year-old's grief. He briefly wondered how he could still feel pain now that he was no longer alive, but had no time to dwell on that since Franky was speaking again.

"Okay. We'll go with you," Franky announced. "But you'd better not be lying to us."

For an instant, Gabriel felt genuine fear. He'd never had a child threaten him with such vehemence. Finding these children a home seemed easy. Gabriel had a fool-proof plan. He knew precisely where they needed to go. It was the getting there that raised the problem.

"First of all, we'll need to get your things," Gabriel announced and each of the children held out a collection of bags that contained all their earthly belongings. Even the youngest shoved his button in his pocket long enough to hoist up a tattered old carpet bag that was nearly as big as he was.

"We have everything," Franky announced grabbing his younger brother's bag.

It saddened Gabriel to think that everything the children owned could be carried in that collection of old sacks.

"Good, then let's head out before Miss Sneathen comes out," Gabriel said, then regretted his words.

"You mean Miss Sneathen doesn't know about you taking us?" Jenny asked.

"No," Gabriel admitted. "Not exactly."

All four of the children hesitated while Franky considered Gabriel's admission.

"Let's go," Franky finally said. "I never liked Miss Sneathen anyway."

"She reminds me of the witch in that movie," Carrie said as they all hurried into the elevator.

"I agree," Gabriel said herding the children into the elevator. "She looks just like Miss Gulch."

Once they arrived at the ground floor, Gabriel led the children to the main entrance of the hospital. Then he was faced with the realization that he didn't have a plan to get everyone from the hospital in Carson Creek to the Canfield farm near Belleview Grange. Then Gabriel recalled that a guardian could have whatever he needed to achieve his goal. Gabriel wondered if that included transportation.

"It sure would be handy to have a car right now," Gabriel muttered under his breath.

Immediately a dark red 1939 Ford Deluxe V-8 drove up to the curb and a young man got out and tossed the keys to Gabriel. Without a moment of hesitation, Gabriel helped the children stash their bags in the trunk. Button and his sisters climbed in the back, while Franky sat up front with Gabriel. No one questioned the miraculous arrival of a car the very moment Gabriel requested it.

Without hesitation, Gabriel pulled away from the curb and headed down the road.

"Where are we going?" Franky asked.

"To a farm just outside Belleview Grange," Gabriel said, then realized there was another flaw in his otherwise perfect plan.

Gabriel grew up as an only child because after his birth and his twin sister's death, his mother couldn't have any more children. It was because of his mother's frustration at being unable to conceive again that he had decided to be a doctor…an OB-GYN. How a doctor who hoped to specialize in female infertility would up on Omaha Beach was beyond Gabriel's powers of reason. But he turned up there, only to end up here with four children that he was certain his parents would be delighted to raise. The problem was, how was he going to show up on their doorstep at just about the same time they'd be getting the news that he'd died in Normandy?

"I probably should have thought this out better," Gabriel muttered to himself.

"Do you always talk to yourself?" Franky asked.

"Yeah," Gabriel admitted. "It helps me figure things out."

Just then Gabriel heard Rachel's voice in his ear. *I know what you're doing, and it won't work,* she said.

"Okay. What am I doing?" Gabriel asked.

"Darned if I know," Franky replied.

"Not you, Franky," Gabriel interrupted. "I'm talking to someone else now."

You can't contact your parents since you haven't officially crossed over, Rachel said. *If you try to speak to them, they won't know you. You'll appear to be someone totally different. If you insist that you're their son, it will only upset them, and may prevent them from accepting the McKinney children for adoption.*

"But they'll be the best option for these kids," Gabriel insisted then noticed Franky staring at him, while noting three pairs of wide eyes in the backseat through the rearview mirror. "I mean, you kids. They'll be the best option for you kids. I'm taking you to this really amazing couple."

I agree, Rachel conceded. *Your parents will be an ideal choice for these children, but you have to be very careful not to reveal who you really are.*

They traveled on, mostly in silence for about a half hour before Carrie began singing and the others chimed in, except Button. Gabriel recognized the song as the one the children had been singing in the hospital. The same song that Angelica had been singing to him on Omaha Beach.

Gabriel realized the song was bolstering their courage at a time when they must have felt terrified. They were all alone in the world, traveling to an unknown destination with a strange man who talked to himself.

"How much further?" Franky asked when the song ended.

"Not long now," Gabriel answered as he turned off the main road on to a dirt track.

Franky looked grim when he realized they had stopped in a field at the edge of a pond.

"Where are we?" Franky demanded. "I thought you were going to take us to our new home. This is the middle of nowhere."

"We're just going to pull off for a few minutes so we can stretch our legs," Gabriel said.

"And then how far?" Franky's jaw jutted out as he scrambled out of the car and assumed a stubborn pose.

"It's right over there," Gabriel said gently taking Franky by the shoulders and turning him around.

Gabriel felt his breath catch as he saw his boyhood home visible across the field. It was a cream-colored farmhouse with a grey roof and hunter green shutters. Behind was a big red barn and a nearby chicken coop. From where Gabriel stood, he could see clean laundry fluttering in the breeze on the line out back.

"Looks like they're home," Franky observed. "Let's go."

"Wait," Gabriel said as he tried to temper the urge he knew he'd experienced when he saw his mother for the first time in months. "We need to strategize."

"What?" Franky demanded. "Do these people know anything about us? Are they really willing to adopt us all or were you just making that up?"

By this time all four of the McKinney children had gotten out of the car and were pinning him with accusing glares.

"They don't know about you yet," Gabriel confessed. "But when they meet you, I just know they're going to fall in love with you."

"How do you know that?" Jenny asked.

"Let's just say I know about these folks and they love kids," Gabriel said. "They had a son, but he died in the war like your dad. So they're grieving just like you. You kids would be doing them a huge favor by helping them heal and keeping them from being lonely. And they'll do everything they can to give you a great childhood."

The children weighed Gabriel's impassioned words then Franky stepped forward to speak for the rest of them.

"Okay. We'll do it," he said. "Now what is this

strategize stuff?"

"We need an excuse for just showing up out of nowhere," Gabriel said trying to come up with a reason for them to drive in unannounced at the Canfield farmhouse.

"How about a flat tire?" Carrie suggested.

"Brilliant!" Gabriel grinned and was about to turn the tire valve enough to cause a slow release of pressure when there was sudden blood curdling scream.

Gabriel could hear a ringing in his ears when the first screech ended only to be followed shortly after by another deafening shriek. He had determined the shrill wail was coming from Button just in time to muffle the third howl by cupping his hand over the boy's mouth.

"What the devil's gotten into him?" Gabriel asked.

"His button," Jenny cried. "He's lost his button."

"Holy cow," Gabriel sighed. "All that noise over a button?"

When four pair of McKinney eyes glared at him, Gabriel recalled the significance of the missing treasure.

"Okay. Spread out. We have to find the button," Gabriel amended.

After searching for minutes with no success, Gabriel made certain none of the children was close to him, then called upon one of his recently acquired skills.

"I could really use that coat button about now," he said, and the missing button rolled up to his left shoe.

After amazed surprise, Gabriel snatched the leather button and held it out.

"Found it," he announced, and the McKinney

children all gathered around him to see.

The five-year-old happily retrieved his button and was about to shove it back in his pocket when Gabriel pulled the lad back.

"Wait a minute there," Gabriel said as he reached deep into the boy's pants pocket. "It feels like you're getting a hole in that pocket. We can't risk having you lose this gem again."

Automatically Gabriel reached in under his shirt and pulled out his dog tags. He snapped open the chain, and glanced briefly at the tags. Rachel had warned him about not identifying himself to his parents, and it would be confusing for a child to show up with their son's dog tags hanging around his neck. Gabriel slid off the tags and discarded them in the dirt and then threaded the child's button on the chain and reconnected it.

"There," Gabriel announced. "Now you won't be losing it again. And you'll always have this reminder that you're never alone."

As Gabriel stooped to hang the talisman around the child's neck, Button rushed into Gabriel's arms and hugged him. The force of the embrace nearly knocked Gabriel over.

Gabriel was so moved by Button's affection that he nearly forgot his plan. When he finally recalled, he went to the left front tire and released the tire stem slightly.

"Okay, come on, kids," Gabriel said. "Let's all get back in the car. We've got a farmhouse to go to and if we're lucky, Mrs. Canfield is about to make lunch."

Moments later, Gabriel pulled into his parent's driveway. His words stuck in his throat as he explained to his father that his tire was going flat, and wondered if there was a pump handy. It hurt that his father didn't recognize him, but that was the bargain he made. Gabriel blinked back tears when his mother came out the back door when she heard the McKinney kids playing out in the yard.

"You children, you come in now," she announced. "Walt and I were just about to have some lunch and we have plenty. Come on, now."

To anyone else, she would have seemed to be a friendly generous farm wife, happily urging guests to join in a meal, but Gabriel sensed a hint of melancholy. When he entered the kitchen, he knew why. He noticed his mother blot tears on her apron as she scooped up a telegram from the kitchen table and shove it in her apron pocket. He realized his parents had just been informed of his death. No matter. The Canfields had company, and they were determined to make them feel welcome.

Gabriel smelled the fresh bread when he walked through the door. He knew his mother must have been up early to start the bread, and it had likely come out of the oven about a half hour ago. His mother rushed about pulling down extra plates and silverware. As soon as she brought them out, Jenny and Carrie quickly set the table. Cheese and bread were sliced, and Gabriel automatically reached in the larder for a big jar of his mother's canned applesauce. He felt a stab of guilt at having almost given himself away, but his mother didn't seem to notice. She simply took the applesauce from him and poured it into a green glass bowl and stuck a big serving spoon in.

A large pot of fresh chicken rice soup simmered on the stove and after prayers, Gabriel's mother began to ladle out bowls of soup that Franky happily passed out to everyone at the table. Gabriel couldn't help but notice that the McKinney children just all dug in and helped without even being asked, and seemed to know what to do as if this was routine.

"Now what brings you lovely children by to see us today?" Helen Canfield asked as she finally took her seat and smiled at the surprise guests that were seated around her table.

"Our Mama died," Franky said before Gabriel had a chance to explain.

They clearly should have spent a little more time strategizing before they arrived at the Canfield farm.

"Gabriel said you'd adopt us," Jenny added.

No doubt about it. Gabriel should have explained to the children that they'd need to refrain from blurting out their plan.

"Gabriel," Mrs. Canfield sighed holding her right hand to her chest. "Your name is Gabriel?"

"Yes, ma'am," he said troubled by the sorrow in his mother's eyes.

Helen Canfield arose abruptly and went to stand by the sink with her back to the table.

"You must excuse my wife," Walt Canfield said softly. "We just received a wire yesterday morning informing us that our son, Gabriel, died on Omaha Beach."

Without a word, Button slipped down from his chair and rushed to her side. He quickly slipped off the chain from around his neck and pressed it with the button into Helen Canfield's hand.

"What's this, sweetheart," she asked stooping down to be at eye level with the five-year-old.

Gabriel quickly explained that the button was the

only thing the child had to remember his father by and that it was supposed to symbolize that he was never alone.

"I think he wants you to have it so you won't be sad about losing your son," Franky added.

"Oh no, darling, I couldn't take your gift," Helen Canfield said returning the chain around the boy's neck. "But that was so kind of you to offer."

Helen escorted Button back to his seat at the table then brought a tray of glasses and a pitcher of lemonade back to the table when she returned.

"It's just been so lonely out here since our Gabriel left for the service," Helen said while she poured up glasses and the children passed them around the table. "We certainly could use some cheer around here, and there's nothing like the sound of children to restore the soul."

"Are you really looking for a home for these young ones?" Walt asked.

"Yes," Gabriel said. "If I can't find a home for them then they're likely to be separated. They were all out at separate foster homes when their mother got too sick to care for them. They had been promised that when the time came, they would be placed all together, but their caseworker admitted that wasn't going to happen."

"What exactly would we have to do to keep these children?" Helen asked before her husband could object.

"Uh, I think you need to sign some papers," Gabriel said, guessing since he didn't have a clue.

You'll find official documents in the car, Gabriel heard Rachel say.

"I have documents in the car," Gabriel added.

And they'll need to be filed with the county and signed by an official of the court.

"And they'll need to be filed with the county and signed by an official of the court," Gabriel added.

"Judge Farley will be at the memorial service tonight," Helen said giving her husband a hopeful smile.

"Then by all means, we'd like to sign those papers and make it official," Walt said grinning back to his wife.

"That is if it's all right with you young folks," Helen said.

Without a word, all the McKinney children rushed to hug Helen. When tears threatened to fall, Gabriel decided to hurry out to the car to figure out where those official documents were that Rachel had mentioned. When he got to the car, he found Rachel waiting.

"That couldn't have been easy," she said with grudging respect.

"But it was the right thing to do," Gabriel said brushing away his tears. "Those kids will help my parents forget the pain of my death, and my parents will give the children the best childhood they could ever want."

"You'd better get back in there," Rachel said. "You only have a little more time."

The rest of the afternoon Helen Canfield showed the children pictures of her son growing up. The girls helped with preparing supper and Gabriel and Franky helped Walt with the farm chores. In the evening, they went to the Mother of Mercy Church for the memorial for Gabriel Canfield where friends and neighbors consoled Helen and Walt and where the

Canfield's got a chance to introduce their new children to their friends. Judge Farley was there and agreed to process the adoption papers.

As the memorial was ending, Gabriel noticed Rachel waiting in the dimly lit parking lot outside the church. He knew it was time for him to leave. He had to admit this had been a surreal evening. There aren't many who get to attend their own funerals...or maybe there were, and Gabriel had never heard about it before. He said a quick goodbye to his parents, fighting the urge to kiss his mother one more time. When she hugged him, he hugged her back. That had to be enough, he reasoned.

Then it came time to say goodbye to the McKinneys.

"Thanks for keeping your word," Franky said putting his hand out for Gabriel to shake.

"My pleasure," Gabriel said.

"Yes, thank you, thank you," the girls chimed in.

"I know who you are," Button said to the astonishment of his siblings. "The lady is waiting for you," he added. "You'd better go."

"What lady?" Franky asked.

"The one over there," Button said pointing at Rachel.

"I don't see any lady," Franky sputtered. "Come on, Button. You're tired. You need to go to bed."

***

"And off they went," Gabriel said to Father Drew. "I never saw them after that, but knowing my folks, they had a great childhood."

"What a lovely recollection," Father Drew said smiling with satisfaction. "I hope my first transition turns out to be as successful and memorable as that one was."

CHAPTER 6

"I've completed the changes to your will."

Gabriel and the priest were startled by the sudden interruption.

"Oh, Timothy," Father Drew said with a broad grin. "This is my friend, Gabriel. We've just been having a pleasant chat. Gabriel, this is my great-nephew, Timothy."

"I'm sorry to intrude, but I just stopped by the library next door and updated your will, then printed out a new copy," Timothy said while sorting through some documents in his briefcase. "You said you were in a hurry, so I just came right back for your signature."

"You're a good kid, Timmy." Father Drew gladly took the will. He glanced over the changes and nodded his approval before he took a pen from his great-nephew and signed and initialed the pages.

"And now you're all set." Timothy loaded the papers back in his briefcase. "I'll leave you two to your visit."

"No wait, Timmy." Father Drew put his right hand out to halt the young man while reaching around his neck. "I've been carrying this medal around for you. It's your patron saint medal. I got one for all the nieces and nephews and yours is the last one. St. Timothy, the Bishop of Ephesus. Something to remember your old great-uncle by."

The young man leaned in while the priest draped the silver medal around his neck.

"There's no chance of forgetting you, Uncle Drew," Timothy said before giving the old priest a hug. "Gotta go. I have a couple last minute Christmas things to pick up."

"Oh Timmy, what have I always told you about putting things off to the last minute?" Father Drew asked.

"You said, *Timmy, do as I say, don't do as I do.*"

"Right," Father Drew agreed. "I should have gotten your patron saint medal to you weeks ago and had my will updated last year. But here I am on my death bed trying to get everything finished at the last minute."

"I find it hard to believe you're at death's door, Uncle Drew," the lawyer scoffed.

"Well, you never know," the priest shrugged while winking at Gabriel.

"If you are on the way out, it doesn't seem to be troubling you," Timothy said as he made his way to the door.

"I've had a grand life," the priest declared. "But if it's time to go, I'm prepared to see what the next great adventure will be."

"Ah yes, *the next great adventure,*" Gabriel repeated after the lawyer left. "I think Duffy is going to be delighted to welcome you to The After."

"So when can I expect this to happen?" Father Drew asked.

"It happens when it happens," Gabriel said. "We'll just wait and see."

"In the meantime, I'd like you to tell me about some of the other people you've transitioned to The After."

"I've already told you about some of my transitions," Gabriel said stretching out in the chair next to the priest's bed. "Tell me more about you. Tell me about your family."

"There's not much to tell," Father Drew admitted. "My contemporaries have all died, so now I just have nieces and nephews and grand-nieces and nephews. Seventeen all together. I ordered each of them a patron saint medal as a remembrance. It gives me comfort to think that they'll have each other to depend upon. Family is important. Take Timothy, for instance. He just graduated from law school and passed the bar within the last couple of years. He doesn't have a huge client list yet, but all his siblings and cousins give him their business. And I have been known to amend my will from time to time."

A moment later, Rachel knocked gently on the door and asked if she could speak to Gabriel alone.

"I'll be right back," Gabriel winked. "Don't leave without me."

"Gabriel, I have a client, and I need your help." Rachel, who was usually the epitome of unflappable calm, looked desperate.

"I'm kind of busy with Father Drew."

"Yes, I know, but I can't leave Sherry right now," Rachel said turning toward the room next door.

"She's about to wake up, and someone needs to be with her."

"Is there no family here?" Gabriel asked.

"A husband. That's who I need help with," Rachel sighed.

"What's wrong?" Rachel's desperation was raising concern in Gabriel.

"It's a long story," Rachel whispered. "Sherry had a brain tumor. For a long time, her insurance company stalled about paying for chemo treatments and ultimately about the surgical technique needed to afford her the best chance at survival."

"So she's dying because she didn't get treatment in time?" Gabriel assumed.

"No, actually, Sherry's surgery was miraculously successful, no thanks to Olympia United Health Insurance." Rachel's last words came out with in a bitter sneer.

"Then what's the problem?" Gabriel asked.

"Earlier in the procedure, things were not looking good for Sherry," Rachel explained. "Her husband has been fighting so long with the insurance company and blames them for Sherry's critical condition. When Mike heard earlier that the procedure was going poorly, he snapped."

"I suppose that's understandable," Gabriel nodded.

"Yes, but Mike was in the military, and he was a munitions and explosives expert," Rachel explained. "When he heard that the doctors didn't expect Sherry to survive the surgery, Mike decided he didn't have anything left to live for."

"Damn. Another suicide," Gabriel muttered.

"Worse," Rachel said. "Mike intends to set off an

explosion at the insurance company's headquarters. You need to stop him, Gabriel. And you need to tell him that Sherry is going to be fine. The procedure was successful after all."

As Rachel completed her plea, Gabriel felt a tingling in his hands and feet. In a blink of the eye, he found himself in a strange corridor. There was a golden glow emanating from a door a few yards away.

When Gabriel passed through the door, he was in an underground parking ramp. The lighting was dim, but he could see from a golden glow where the man he sought was located.

"Hi, Mike. I'm Gabriel. We need to talk." Gabriel's greeting came out calm but urgent.

The desperate man near a support pillar rummaged around in one of his large canvas bags. When he pulled out a gun and aimed it at Gabriel, he expected a much different reaction than Gabriel's chuckle.

"Who the hell are you?" the man demanded.

"I told you, I'm Gabriel, and I'm here to give you a message."

"I'm not interested in messages," Mike smirked. "I'm kind of busy here."

"Yeah. You may wish to reconsider this," Gabriel said coming close even as Mike raised the gun and aimed at Gabriel's heart, at least to the place his heart used to be.

"You can't hurt me," Gabriel smiled. "I'm already dead, but if you don't stop what you're doing, you will be too."

"That's the plan," Mike sneered. "By now, my Sherry is dead, so I've got no reason to go on. But if I'm dying, I'm taking Olympia United Health with me."

"You don't want to do this. For one thing, Sherry isn't dead, and isn't likely to die anytime soon," Gabriel explained.

"You're lying," Mike cried out. "I heard the surgeon say there was nothing they could do. Sherry couldn't be saved."

"There's been a change in prognosis," Gabriel insisted. "Sherry is going to survive, and don't you think she's going to want to see you when she comes out of anesthesia?"

"Get out of here," Mike warned. "I'm busy."

"Look, Mike, you need to believe me, your wife is not going to die. And she's going to need you," Gabriel repeated. "Besides, this isn't you. Maybe you don't care if you die, but there are others to consider."

"It's Christmas Eve," Mike pointed out. "There's no one here but me. All I'm going to do is take out their headquarters and call attention to all the ways they withhold vital treatment from desperately ill people."

"No, you're not alone." Gabriel glanced up sensing a number of other souls in the building. "There are a handful of people on the sixth floor who have no family in town who are celebrating Christmas with an impromptu office party. There are cleaning crews dispatched on every floor and several security guards patrolling throughout the building."

"Yeah and one of those security guards may be showing up any minute so I have work to do," Mike snapped.

"You really don't want to be responsible for hurting or killing those people, Mike." Gabriel's soothing logic finally got to Mike.

After a few moments, Mike lowered the gun.

"Who the hell are you?" Mike asked again.

Please hurry. Gabriel alone heard Rachel's plea.

"I'm a Guardian of Transitions," Gabriel said, then considered how most people seemed unimpressed with that title. "I'm the *freaking Angel of Death*, and if you don't do as I say, you're going to die. I'm going to have to take you to the hereafter while your beloved wife will become a widow and have to face guilt over your useless death and the loss of the others you will be responsible for harming. Is that what you really want, Mike?"

Even though Mike still held his weapon, he stepped back in fear from the growing rage in Gabriel's glowing eyes.

"Are you sure my Sherry is going to be all right?" Mike demanded as he shoved his gun back into one of his canvas bags.

"She will be if she wakes up in recovery and finds you next to her bed," Gabriel said placing a comforting hand on Mike's shoulder. "Come on. We need to get back to the hospital now."

Gabriel helped Mike reload the explosives and fuses back in the bags. Once the supplies were secured, Gabriel grabbed one bag while Mike picked up the other. They were just about to place the bags in the trunk of Mike's car, when a security guard stopped them.

"This is the executive parking ramp," the guard announced. "I don't see an official sticker on your windshield. I don't suppose you have a permit on you?"

"Uh, yes I do," Gabriel said miraculously producing an official permit for the guard to examine.

"A guest pass."

After checking out the permit, the guard noticed the suspicious cargo that he'd witnessed Gabriel and Mike place in the still open trunk.

"What are you carrying in those bags?" the guard asked.

"Uh, kittens," Gabriel said with a grin, while Mike had a look of panic on his face. "I got a call from one of the senior sales staff that some stray cat decided to have her kittens down here a while ago, and they've been making themselves at home. He wanted the momma and her brood out of here ASAP before this parking ramp started smelling like one big litter box."

"Kittens?" the guard broke out in a broad smile. "Hey, could I have one of those kittens? I've got a granddaughter that'd love a new kitten for Christmas."

"Sure," Gabriel agreed and leaned in to unzip one of the bags while Mike's anxiety erupted, and he decided to make a run for it.

"What's with him?" the guard asked as Gabriel handed him a squirming furry creature from the bag that had moments before contained Mike's gun and various explosive devices.

"He's allergic," Gabriel shrugged. "So which one do you want? We have mostly gray tigers, but there's one solid gray."

"This one's a beauty," the guard said taking one of the tigers. "My granddaughter's going to think she's got the best granddad in the world."

"I'm sure she will," Gabriel agreed. "Come on, Mike. It's safe to come back. I've got all the kittens back in the bag."

"You guys have a Merry Christmas now," the

guard said as he happily walked off with his squealing kitten.

Mike returned, astounded by what he'd just witnessed.

"How'd you do that?" he asked.

"*Angel of Death*, remember?" Gabriel grinned. "Actually, we call ourselves the Guardians of Transitions, because if we're very lucky, people don't actually die. We simply help them transition from a sometimes dark terrifying place, back to a new normal. That's what happened here tonight. You agreed to listen, and I could help you. And now we need to get to Sherry so you can be there for her when she awakens."

"What about the kittens?" Mike asked.

"What kittens?"

"You gave the guard a kitten," Mike said opening the bag Gabriel had just zipped closed. When he looked inside, the bag was empty.

"Guardians are given whatever they need to help with their client," Gabriel shrugged. "I needed a parking pass and a few kittens. Occasionally, I actually require cars, so this assignment was relatively easy."

"What happened to the explosives?" Mike demanded.

"Oh, you don't need those now," Gabriel explained. "And besides, it's illegal to have some of that stuff. You wouldn't want to be caught with that in your vehicle. Now, back to the hospital."

Mike and Gabriel got in Mike's car and as they were backing out, he said, "I was just thinking, Sherry might want one of those kittens."

"I'll see what I can do."

CHAPTER 7

When they arrived at the hospital, Mike rushed into his wife's room, just as she opened her eyes.

"I love you, Sherry," Mike said leaning in to kiss her forehead. "You're going to be fine, Baby. We're going to be fine."

Rachel quietly backed out of the room and gently closed the door behind her.

"He won't remember anything about going to the insurance company to place bombs, or anything about your intervention," Rachel said. "All he'll recall is that he was angry enough to commit the crimes, but reconsidered when he heard that Sherry would survive."

Gabriel nodded in understanding. Over the past seventy-five years most of his successful human contacts did not remember their experience with him. He was simply the good Samaritan that came to their aid, or the disembodied voice of reason that put clever ideas into their minds that miraculously solved previously impossible situations. Even if he seemed

physically present in their lives, he would soon be
forgotten once his assignment was completed.
Turning back to Father Drew's room, he was
intrigued by what the priest had said earlier.

Father Drew had been expecting Gabriel. He said
that others had spoken of Gabriel…or someone
described him as the kindly visitor who came with
reassurances at the time of death. It would seem that
some people did not forget his missions. That
dichotomy intrigued him.

"Rachel, why do some remember us and others
forget?" Gabriel asked.

"Some people simply need some guidance, a push
in the right direction," Rachel explained. "When
we've finished, it seems best to let them believe they
came to their decisions on their own. It reinforces for
them, the strength that they can trust their judgement.
And afterward, many times they can make wiser
choices."

"And what about the ones who do remember?"
Gabriel asked.

"It's kind of like the people who see us even when
we may not show ourselves," Rachel said
philosophically. "Quite often the young and innocent
see us when others don't. Those who remember us
obviously need to remember. They need to believe
there is a system that reaches out to them in time of
need and helps them. Even when the outcome is not
good, they know they are never alone, never
abandoned. It's a truly honorable and rewarding gift
for us to serve those who need our help."

"Father Drew said he expected me," Gabriel said
as he began to make his way back to the priest's
room. "He said others have spoken about seeing me

comforting those who are dying. He referred to me as *The Angel of Death*."

As expected, Rachel rolled her eyes at the mention of the phrase.

"I know we aren't supposed to call ourselves angels," Gabriel quickly added, "And that the term *Angel of Death* sometimes has a negative connotation, but today I told Sherry's husband, Mike, that is who I was and it really got his attention.

"Well, calling undue attention to ourselves isn't what we're supposed to be doing," Rachel pointed out. "It's probably best that Mike forgets you."

"Yeah, I guess so." Gabriel knew he should put Mike out of his mind as well. It was gratifying at least one of his clients had survived Christmas Eve, and Gabriel was happy it could be Mike.

"You'd better be getting back to Father Drew," Rachel said as she turned to leave. "Oh, by the way, I looked in on him while you were gone. He mentioned his great-nephew was an attorney, and suggested that he'd be available to represent Sherry and Mike against the insurance company. It seems they aren't the only people who have been victimized by Olympia."

Gabriel grinned with satisfaction when he entered Father Drew's room, but his good spirits faded when he noticed the priest was grimacing in pain. Automatically, Gabriel reached for the call button to summon a nurse.

"Father Drew needs help immediately," Gabriel said grasping the priest's hand.

"It's no good." Father Drew took a slow deep breath, then slowly released it. "I think this may be the end."

"It doesn't mean you have to suffer," Gabriel said

as he moved out of the way when the nurse came in.

"I have your pain meds," the nurse said as he administered an injection in the priest's IV. "Is there anything else I can do for you, Father?"

"No, I'll be fine," the priest said with a forced smile. "You'd best get home, Fred. It's Christmas Eve and your young wife and baby are going to wonder where you are."

The nurse nodded and left.

Gabriel pulled a chair up to the bed and held the priest's hand.

"Relax now. Be calm and believe and soon this will pass," Gabriel said.

"But I have one more question," the priest said while trying to ignore the pain in his chest. "Christmas is such a happy time, yet the holiday does not seem to bring you joy. What is it about this holiday that troubles you?"

Gabriel closed his eyes wishing he could ignore Father Drew's observation, but it was true. Christmas had been a difficult time for him. He could deny it, but he realized the priest would probably see through any lame excuses he might offer. And yet Gabriel tried.

"Well, Christmas is just another workday for me," Gabriel began, noticing the old priest arched his left brow. "No honestly," Gabriel continued. "And around the holidays, people just do stupid things. It seems they're more idiotic than the whole rest of the year. Remember, so far today, I had a suicide, a guy who wouldn't listen and accidentally killed himself, and just now a guy who was going to blow up a building."

"I'm not buying it," Father Drew said.

"Remember, I'm in the business of confessions, and I've heard a lot of crap and excuses in my life. What's the real reason that Christmas leaves you so bitter and cynical?"

With a deep sigh, Gabriel gave in.

"A little more than a year before I died, I was home on leave during the Christmas holidays," he began. "On Christmas Eve I asked my girlfriend to marry me. I gave her a ring and she happily agreed assuming we'd just find the nearest judge and say the vows."

"And something prevented it?" Father Drew asked when Gabriel paused.

"I didn't believe it was prudent to marry as long as I was in the service," Gabriel confessed. "I thought it would be better to wait. I didn't want her to be a widow if I didn't make it home."

"And apparently she didn't agree with your assessment," the old priest added when Gabriel paused again.

"No. She didn't agree," Gabriel admitted. "She gave my ring back to my mother after I went back to my regiment. She didn't even have the courtesy to tell me herself. In fact, she married another guy on New Year's Eve, and I found out on the following Christmas that she and her husband had a baby. I heard that from an old high school buddy. She never contacted me at all. So yeah. I'm not big on Christmas."

"That's dreadful, Gabriel," the priest said with sincere sympathy. "What she did was insensitive, but she may just have not had the courage to tell you she'd had second thoughts about your proposal. Some women get caught up in the moment when a man asks to marry them and then on closer examination, realize it might be a mistake."

"I'd dated this girl since high school." Gabriel turned away to hide his pain. "I wanted to get out of school and be able to support her and give her a home. It was a dream I believed we both shared. I guess it was just taking too long, and she didn't want to wait anymore. What I didn't realize was that she'd given up on that dream long before I knew it. While I was working, and going to school, and later when I was in the service, she was dating lots of other guys. My high school friend eventually admitted to me that he found out all about the string of men she'd been seeing. The only reason she accepted my proposal was that she believed she was pregnant at the time. She thought if we got married right away, I wouldn't realize I wasn't the father."

Gabriel let out a frustrated sigh and ran his fingers through his hair before he turned back to the priest.

"It turned out it was a false alarm. She wasn't pregnant." Gabriel sighed. "But she married some other guy before she realized it, and before the end of the year, she did have a baby with him."

"Well, maybe it was a good thing you didn't marry her then," the priest shrugged. "Regardless, you can't blame Christmas for the irresponsible acts of an unfaithful woman."

"I realize that," Gabriel agreed. "I was better off not marrying her. It's just that Christmas always brings those painful memories back to me. Maybe that's why I keep so busy at this time of year. Perhaps it's meant to distract me from that Christmas back in 1942 and help me to move on."

"Yes," the priest grimaced and quickly tried to

hide his pain. "You should move on to more pleasant memories."

"And perhaps you should relax," Gabriel said. It was obvious that the old priest was experiencing more discomfort.

Gabriel arose and stood next to the priest, folding his right hand over Father Drew's folded hands.

He could hear the priest's prayers being recited, though they weren't spoken out loud. A while later, when the doctor arrived to examine him, Father Drew had already passed, and he and Gabriel had left.

"It is a beautiful path, just as you promised," the priest said looking and feeling restored and pain free.

"You're sure you don't want St. Peter and the Pearly Gate?" Gabriel asked. "Because I'm sure Duffy would be happy to get you in."

"No, no. This is perfect," Father Drew insisted.

Gabriel glanced around seeing the flower meadow as he imagined Father Drew was observing it for the first time.

"Oh look there," the priest said excitedly pointing ahead. "That must be your friend, Angelica."

Glancing back, Gabriel noticed the dark-haired girl with the crown of flowers rushing to welcome them.

"Welcome, Andrew," she said skipping with delight. "And welcome back, Gabriel. I missed you."

Father Drew scooped up the child and hugged her while Gabriel observed the priest's easy charm.

"And you must be Duffy," the priest said when he noticed the short chubby Guardian of Welcome. "Gabriel has told me exactly what to expect, and I'm so eager to walk the road of remembrance and see all my friends and family at the end. I can hardly wait."

"Are you certain Gabriel told you that?" Duffy

asked. "As I recall, Gabriel wasn't inclined to do anything like that. He still hasn't made the journey of remembrance or had his reunion."

"Then you must go with me," Father Drew insisted. "Once you see how fantastic this is, I'm sure you'll be eager to do it yourself."

"Come along, Gabriel," Angelica urged.

"You can't say no to this adorable child," Father Drew said setting her down on the path and watching as she hurried down the trail that led into the woods. "Come along."

Reluctantly, Gabriel held back.

"You won't see anything you don't want to see," Duffy whispered. "This is, after all, Andrew's life memories. There's no reason why you can't join him."

Gabriel nodded in understanding and followed after the jubilant priest. Though Gabriel saw nothing of Father Andrew's memories, there was no mistake that the priest was witnessing treasured moments from his past. Before long, they reached a shimmering archway and the priest's face glowed with anticipation.

"Don't stop now," Father Drew begged. "Come with me through the arch."

"No," Gabriel said disappointed that he couldn't witness the people just beyond the arch, since the priest was so eager to join them. "It's not for me, Father. This is for you."

Once again, Gabriel was plunged into the memory of his last day. He recalled passing by all the faces of the dying soldiers and recalled how he'd killed a man just moments before his own death.

"Very well," the priest conceded. "But before I go, I have a gift for you."

The priest reached under his cassock and pulled out a chain from around his neck. Gabriel half expected to be shown an Angel Gabriel medal, but instead the priest pressed something else in his hand.

"This is to remember me by. I don't need it anymore, and it appears you do. This is to remind you that you are never alone."

In an instant, Gabriel heard a cacophony of shouting voices. When he looked up, a young man and two young women were waving joyously.

"Come on, Button. What's taking you so long?" the young man shouted. "Come on, get a move on!"

"Button?" Gabriel repeated. "You're Button?"

The priest grinned as he nodded.

When Gabriel opened his hand, he saw the leather button from seventy-five years before on the chain he'd removed his dog tags from.

"You have to come, Gabriel," the priest implored. "Our parents are calling us."

Only then did Gabriel see his mother and father with the adult McKinney children.

"Hurry, Gabriel," Angelica said grabbing his hand. "Momma can't wait to see you."

"Momma?" Gabriel asked.

"You didn't know that Angelica was your twin sister?" the priest asked.

"No." Gabriel felt tears of joy come to his eyes as he was overcome with emotion.

"Well, it's about time you finally crossed into the fulfillment," Duffy said from behind him. It's only taken seventy-five years, but you'll finally celebrate Christmas with your family again."

Gabriel felt overwhelmed by the love of his family and all those whose lives he had touched, including his parents and sister, all the McKinneys who had passed to The After, all the soldiers he had saved and helped, all his friends who had passed before him and every soul he'd ever transitioned.

"Merry Christmas, indeed." Gabriel whispered in awe.

***

After a joyful reunion for Gabriel and Father Drew, it was time to help the priest assume his new role as a Guardian of Transitions. For the first time, Gabriel was a trusted mentor to a new recruit. Gabriel painstakingly went over the rules, regarding the duties of office.

"Remember, whatever you need to accomplish your assignment will be provided," Gabriel said. "You'll recognize your assigned person because they'll glow. You go in invisible and observe. Then you can remain unseen and just be a voice in their head, or if necessary, you can appear before them. You'll get a feel for what works best as you get used to the job. But you'll do great, Father. You're a natural. And if you screw up, they'll just forget you were ever there."

Gabriel stayed with Father Drew as he felt drawn to his first client. They found themselves in a familiar parking lot, outside St. Luke's Hospital. Coming through the doors were Mike and Sherry whom Gabriel had met on Christmas Eve.

"Okay, Father, these are your clients," Gabriel began. "I've told you about this couple. Sherry is recovering from surgery and she requires some rehab. She'll need you to encourage her and keep her spirits up, and Mike will need a steady hand as he pursues the lawsuit against the insurance company. And remember, your great-nephew is representing them. Since you've already passed into fulfillment, Timothy may recognize you, so it might be best not to be visible too much. They all need guidance. Got it?"

Father Drew nodded in understanding and went off to catch up with his new clients.

"That was very good advice," Rachel said as she drew near Gabriel. "You've really mellowed out and matured as a guardian since you passed over into the fulfillment."

"Yeah, right. But I have to go," Gabriel interrupted.

"What are you doing?" Rachel asked as she watched Gabriel rush off to follow Father Drew.

"I just remembered," Gabriel called back. "I owe these people a kitten."

The End

ABOUT THE AUTHOR

P.L. Klein has been writing for publication since 2010. Besides being a prolific author of Romance, Paranormal, Science Fiction, Mystery and Suspense, she is a gifted Watercolorist, Pen and Ink illustrator and pencil sketch artist. She's a lifelong resident of West Michigan, though she's traveled extensively throughout the US and Europe. The best part of living where she does with her husband is that she's near her children and grandchildren.

Also by P. L. Klein

Then Home I'll Be
Juneberry And The Tall Dark Stranger
The Boy Who Danced With Monkeys
Voices In The Mirror
In The Shadow Of The Mind's Eye
Living In The Shadows
Rising From The Shadows
The Vitruvian Deceptions
Secrets Of Dragon Back Ridge

Made in the USA
Middletown, DE
21 July 2019